WORK

For my kids, Montalto Sweet
and Nino Paul Hallelujah
SF

For Levi, with love from Tati
JR

Text copyright © 2024 by Shaina Feinberg
Illustrations copyright © 2024 by Julia Rothman
Design by Jenny Volvovski

Additional copyright acknowledgments appear on page 62.

First edition 2024

Library of Congress Catalog Card Number pending
ISBN 978-1-5362-3266-0

24 25 26 27 28 29 APS 10 9 8 7 6 5 4 3 2 1

Printed in Humen, Dongguan, China

This book was typeset in New Century Schoolbook.
The illustrations were done in mixed media.

Candlewick Press
99 Dover Street
Somerville, Massachusetts 02144

www.candlewick.com

WRK

Interviews with People Doing Jobs They Love

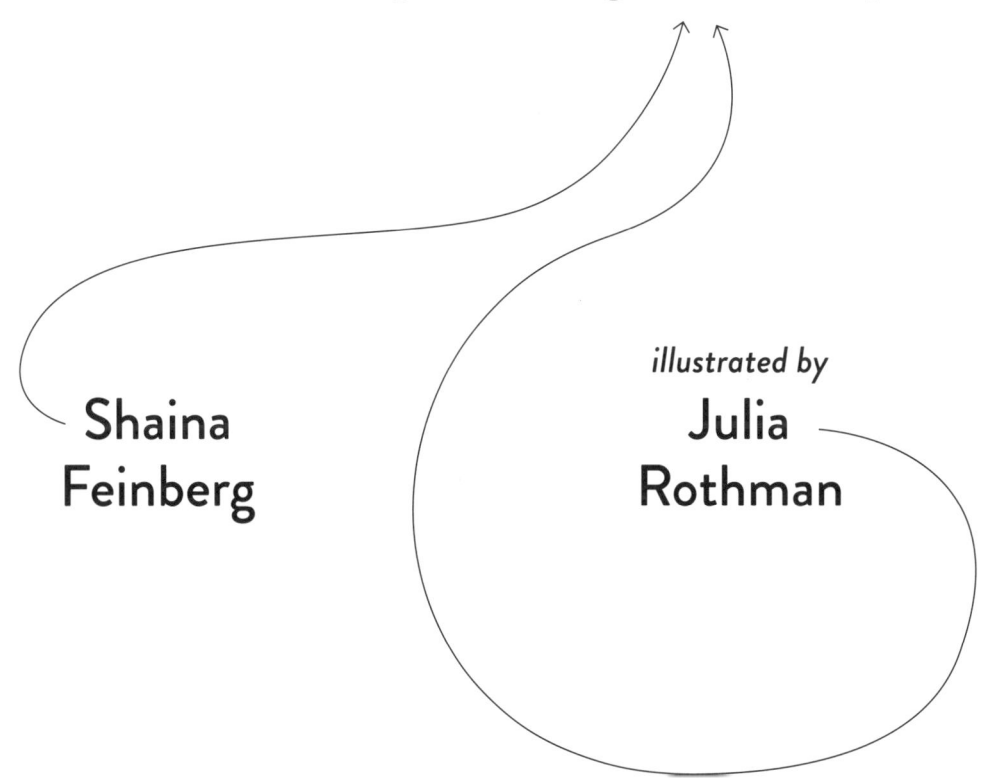

Shaina
Feinberg

illustrated by
Julia
Rothman

CANDLEWICK PRESS

In this book, you will find people from all over the world doing all kinds of jobs. As you look through the pages, you will meet people who are fixing cars and instruments, growing food and flowers, protecting our wildlife, making things easier for others, and inspiring us with their words and art.

Contents

Dr. Robert Aruho is a

WILDLIFE VETERINARIAN

in Kampala, Uganda.

In some parts of Uganda, there are very few giraffes left because of **poaching**. One of Dr. Aruho's jobs as a **veterinarian** is to help grow the giraffe population. In order to do this, Dr. Aruho moves giraffes from one location to another. Once the giraffes are in the new location, they will **mate** and make babies.

"Moving a giraffe is quite a delicate procedure," says Dr. Aruho. "They have long necks. They have long legs. There are risks associated with such a tall animal. We have to make sure the animal is safe."

It takes many people to move just one giraffe. "We usually have eleven people," says Dr. Aruho. "One is guiding them in the front, and then we have five people on each side." The people use ropes to help guide the giraffe to a truck.

There are trees in the truck so the giraffes can eat during their journey.

"We only move giraffes once a year because we have to prepare. You can't wake up in the morning and say, 'Tomorrow I am moving a giraffe.'"

Dr. Aruho and his team drive the giraffes to a new location in a truck.

"The moment you see the giraffes come out of the truck, it is a big celebration! It is a great moment because all of the risks have paid off."

? **Do you like taking care of animals?**

Dan Treiber and **Reina Mia Brill** are

TOY SHOP OWNERS

on City Island in the Bronx, New York.

"We sell objects of interest," says Dan. "We rescue old, good things."

 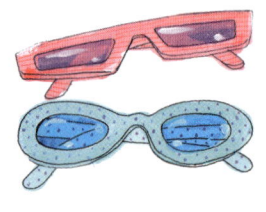

"Mostly we sell **collections**," says Dan. "We sell 1940s **matchbooks**, bottle caps, horse teeth, 1980s baseball cards that are still in their wrappers, unopened packs of trading cards with the stick of gum."

Dan thinks toys should be reused instead of being thrown away. It's better for the environment to make fewer new toys.

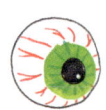 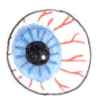

"If you take care of stuff, when you're done with it, someone else can enjoy it," says Dan.

All kinds of people come into the shop—from little kids to the elderly. Adults like buying old toys they'd had when they were young.

"I love making people happy," says Dan. "We sell things that bring people joy. We sell happiness!"

Sometimes artists buy items from the shop and make them into sculptures.

? **Do you collect anything? What do you do with your toys when you are done with them?**

Andini Makosinski <u>is an</u>

INVENTOR

**on Vancouver Island
in Canada.**

"We usually think of **Thomas Edison** or **Nikola Tesla** when we think of an inventor," says Andini. "But I think an inventor can be anyone that just sees things around them and goes, *If I piece them together, can I make something better out of it? Or solve a problem?*"

As a kid, Andini once tried to make a camera out of a cardboard soap box, the chain from a broken necklace, and a bottle cap. It didn't work, but it was fun to make.

oscilloscope
(displays and measures
electronic signals)

power supply

microscope

drill

soldering
iron

Andini invented a
flashlight that runs
off the heat from
someone's hand.

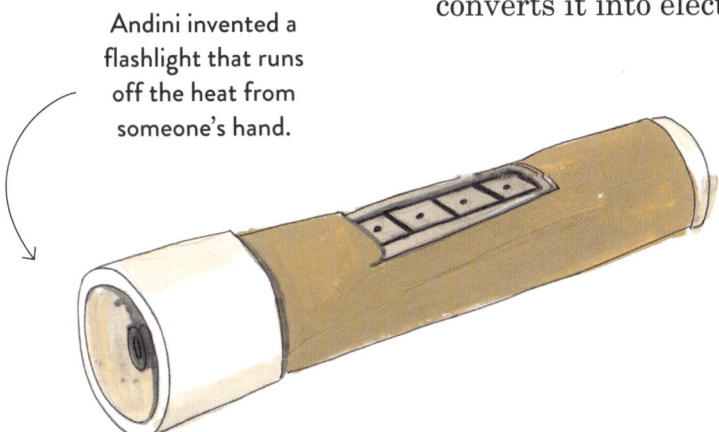

Over time, Andini became most interested in creations that use **alternative energy**. She invented a mug that **harvests** the excess energy from your hot drink and converts it into electricity.

"If we don't use alternative energy sources, we're just using coal and oil and things that are really bad for the environment," says Andini. "The more we can use the energy that's naturally produced around us—like wind, sun, **geothermal** energy, energy from wave movement, heat—the better. Because then we aren't polluting the environment."

? **If you could invent anything, what would it be?**

Pete Kern is a

CANDLESTICK MAKER

in Dromahair, Ireland.

"I always loved candles," says Pete. "I would sit at home reading a good book and have a candle lit."

As a young man, Pete moved to Ireland from Germany. When he moved he couldn't find any good candles, so he started making and selling his own.

At first he made the candles in his living room. "I was messing around, trying things out," says Pete. "My first candles were terrible."

Eventually he succeeded in making nice candles.

All of the candles Pete makes are **beeswax**, which smells like honey. "In one year, I use about six thousand pounds of beeswax," he says.

Pete no longer works from his living room. He has a workshop and a team of candlemakers who help him produce the candles. They make and sell around 30,000 candles a year.

"It is so peaceful to make candles," says Pete. "When we roll the beeswax, it is like meditation."

? **What is something you like to do that is calming?**

Braydon Saunders <u>is a</u>

TOUR GUIDE
at Budj Bim National Park in Victoria, Australia.

Budj Bim is very important to the Gunditjmara people, who are **Aboriginal** Australians. Braydon and his **ancestors** are Gunditjmara.

"Budj Bim was a part of my people's creation story," says Braydon. "The story is that Budj Bim was a spirit being who was as tall as the clouds and he would walk around and create the **landscape**. Eventually, he lay himself down and became the landscape."

Braydon takes visitors on tours of the park and tells them why the land is so special. He also teaches visitors about the Gunditjmara people. "We have the oldest **aquaculture** system in the world," says Braydon. "We created a **sustainable** lifestyle by farming eels and other fish."

Braydon thinks it is important for people all over the world to know about each other's culture. He is happy to be passing down the history of his people and their land.

The Gunditjmara people are famous for farming and eating eels. Braydon demonstrates how an eel basket works for trapping an eel.

Do you know any stories about your ancestors? Is there somewhere important to you that you would like to share with others?

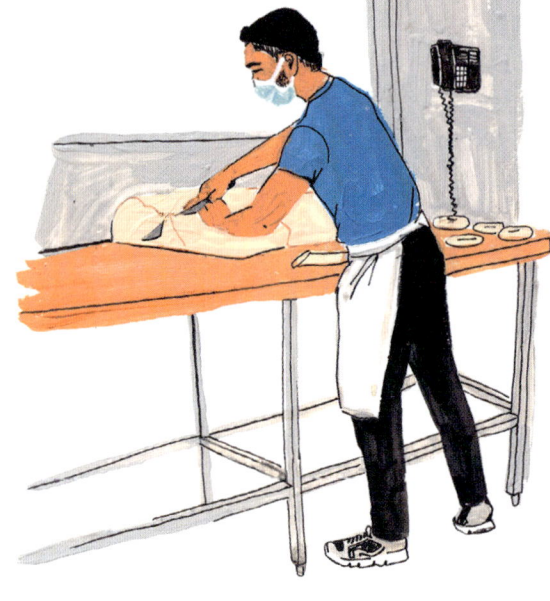

Joe Morena is a

BAGEL BAKER

at St-Viateur Bagel in Montreal, Canada.

"They call me Joe Bagel," says Joe. "I'm the bagel man. I've been baking bagels since I was fourteen."

Bagels are made by rolling dough into a loop and then boiling and baking the dough. Montreal bagels are boiled in honey water to make them sweet.

In Montreal, they speak French. The sign on Joe's store says *The House of Bagel.*

"For the longest time, I only produced two kinds of bagels," says Joe. "Poppy and sesame." Now, St-Viateur makes many kinds of bagels, including one they call "all dressed," otherwise known as an everything bagel—which means it's covered in salt, onion, garlic, poppy seeds, and sesame seeds.

Joe has made a lot of bagels in his life. He has also eaten a lot of bagels. "I like a bagel right out of the oven," says Joe. "I really enjoy my bagel with ricotta and figs on it. Fresh figs."

? **What have you baked? What do you like about baking?**

17

Joana Andrade is a
SURFER
**based in
Ericeira, Portugal.**

Joana has been surfing since she was twelve years old. "When I was young, I got bullied a lot because I was super small," she says. "My parents would try to get me to do sports, like basketball and ballet. They said it would help me get bigger. I tried all kinds of sports but didn't like them. Then, the first time I went to the ocean and got on a surfboard, I knew that was the sport I wanted to do."

In Portugal, the water is cold, so Joana wears a **wet suit** when she surfs.

Some of the waves that Joana surfs are huge. They are the size of three houses stacked on top of each other. "It's like surfing **Mount Everest**. It's a lot of emotions at the same time—it's a mix of adrenaline and fear—but in the end it's like freedom."

Over the years, Joana has won a lot of competitions, and she even became a national champion in Portugal.

Now Joana teaches surfing to kids. She thinks learning to surf is like therapy. "To be in the ocean, you have to live in the moment. You forget the past and the future, you are there one hundred percent!"

? **What do you do that makes you feel like you're living in the moment?**

Linda van der Slot and Marlies Weijers are
FLOWER FARMERS
in Lisse, Holland.

Linda and Marlies love working together: "We are a good team!"

Traditionally, flower farmers grow **bulbs**. They ship the bulbs off to **wholesalers** who sell the bulbs all over the world. "The bulbs go in crates and they go on a truck. The crates of bulbs go somewhere, but you never hear of them again. We said, 'Let's do it differently!'"

Linda and Marlies opened their farm fields to visitors. "When people visit us, they don't just buy flowers and take pictures. We also explain the process of growing the flowers and the importance of the soil and the temperature," Linda says.

Insects love their farm. "In the summer," says Linda, "the dahlia fields are a big playground for bees and butterflies."

Linda and Marlies like seeing how happy the flowers make people.

These are four of the 200 varieties of dahlias grown on the farm.

Fam flower farm

Flower field

Coffee

Chickens

? Have you ever worked with a friend to make something? Have you ever grown anything?

Lauren Nassef is a

RESEARCH ASSISTANT

at the Field Museum in Chicago, Illinois.

"I do lots of different things from day to day," says Lauren. "But pretty much everything I do is to support scientists at the museum to make new research discoveries about nature."

One thing that Lauren does is help care for a collection of specimens. Specimens are organisms—such as plants and animals—used for study. "I have to make sure they are well cared for, organized, and installed to be permanently available to scientists now and into the future," says Lauren.

Lauren was trained as an artist. She has the right set of skills to help scientific researchers do their work. "It turns out, science is a lot about asking questions and then showing what you've discovered." Lauren helps to show these discoveries by photographing specimens and making maps.

Sometimes Lauren has to write really, really small. "In my job interview, they gave me an extra-hard pencil and said, 'Please write the numbers one through nine as tiny as you possibly can.'"

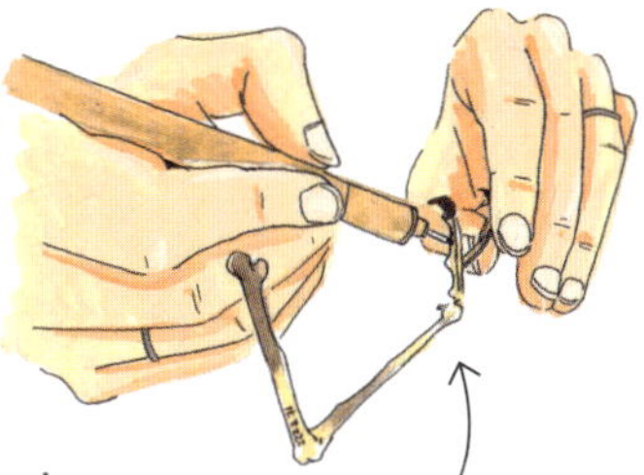

Lauren has to write really small so she can number bones.

A lot of the specimens that Lauren works with are stored in drawers or jars.

? Have you ever collected something from nature—like pine cones or seashells—and then displayed them for someone to see? How small can you write?

Pato Rodriguez is a

STREET FOOD VENDOR

in Buenos Aires, Argentina.

Pato and Romi's food stall was featured on a cooking show. Since being on that show, their tortilla has become **internationally** famous.

She runs a **food stall** in a market with her partner, Romi Moore.

Before Pato, the stall, called Las Chicas de la 3, was run by her mom, dad, and brother. "My family has been doing it forever," says Pato.

Cubed potatoes and eggs are mixed for the tortilla.

The most popular dish that Pato makes is called a **tortilla**. It's made with potato, eggs, ham, and cheese.

"It depends on the number of customers we have," says Pato, "but we use about three or four big bags of potatoes—around one hundred and seventy pounds—and maybe two hundred eggs a day.

"We have all kinds of customers," she says. "We have truckers, vegetable vendors, business executives, and tourists."

Pato loves to cook. She also loves to be in contact with the customers. "It's a real pleasure for us to see our customers' reactions when they eat the food. It's very important to have that connection."

? **Have you ever cooked something that people love to eat? What do you like about cooking?**

Iman Aldebe is a

FASHION DESIGNER

in Stockholm, Sweden.

Ever since she was six years old, Iman knew she wanted to be a fashion designer.

Iman designed the first uniform veil for the Swedish police.

She designs **modest** clothes and **headwear**, like **turbans**. Some women dress modestly and wear a headscarf as part of their religion. Many headscarves are very plain or simple. Iman wanted to create new designs so that women could express themselves in different ways. "My designs make women more visible."

To Iman, it is important to show that Muslim women can be independent and powerful. "I like to make things that are not only pretty," she says. "They also make people think."

When designing clothes, Iman just starts sewing. "I don't like to make sketches ahead of time," she says. "That makes me feel restricted. I like to create every piece not knowing what will happen. That way, each piece is different."

? **How do the clothes you wear make you feel?**

Satoko Ichihara is a **PLAYWRIGHT** in Tokyo, Japan.

"I love to write," says Satoko. "I write plays and I write novels. But writing novels can be very lonely. You're stuck in your room by yourself."

When Satoko writes and directs plays, she is not alone. "With a play," she says, "you work with other people. It's a lot more fun." She especially loves to work with actors. It's exciting to see them perform her work in ways she had not imagined.

Want to write plays? Satoko says, "As you're living your life as a kid, take notes of the things that don't feel right to you. Like the things that you wanted to say and couldn't get out—write those things down and turn them into plays."

Satoko always loved the theater. "When I decided I wanted to be a part of that world," she says, "I thought I would be an actor, because that was what I knew about the theater." But it turned out that Satoko didn't like being an actor.

So, when she was twenty-two, Satoko started casually writing ideas in her cell phone. After a while, she gathered all of the ideas together. She had written a lot! "What I had written added up to a play."

? **What kinds of stories do you like to write?**

The actors stand around a piano to rehearse a scene with singing.

Daniela Ghezzo is a

COBBLER

in Venice, Italy.

Daniela also makes shoes for herself. "I don't have a lot of shoes. I have one for winter and one for summer."

Each pair of **custom-made** shoes that Daniela makes by hand is for a specific person. She meets every single customer and takes their measurements so that the shoes fit them perfectly.

"I need to really understand what they want the shoes for and what kind of life they live," she says.

Before making a pair of shoes, Daniela likes to imagine the shoe and the person it is meant for from all angles.

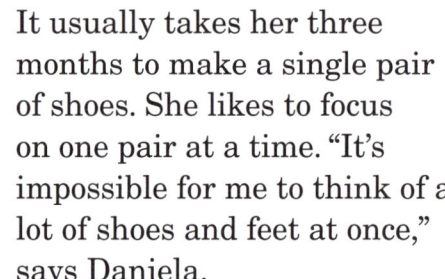

It usually takes her three months to make a single pair of shoes. She likes to focus on one pair at a time. "It's impossible for me to think of a lot of shoes and feet at once," says Daniela.

Daniela doesn't have any sewing machines or stitching machines in her shop. She does everything by hand.

Making shoes by hand is a lot of work. "It's physically difficult," says Daniela. But it feels like the job she was born to do. "My heart is in it."

? What kind of shoe would you make? What is your favorite pair of shoes?

Karen Braitmayer is an

ARCHITECT & ACCESSIBILITY SPECIALIST

in Seattle, Washington.

"I help other architects and building owners make sure that their buildings are as **accessible** as possible to people with disabilities," says Karen. "If you make a building accessible, you're making it easy for everyone to get in the door."

In order to make a building welcoming to all kinds of people, Karen thinks about how different people might move through the building.

"An architect needs to like making things," says Karen. As a kid, Karen made things all the time. She did embroidery, used a sewing machine, and made dollhouses out of shoeboxes.

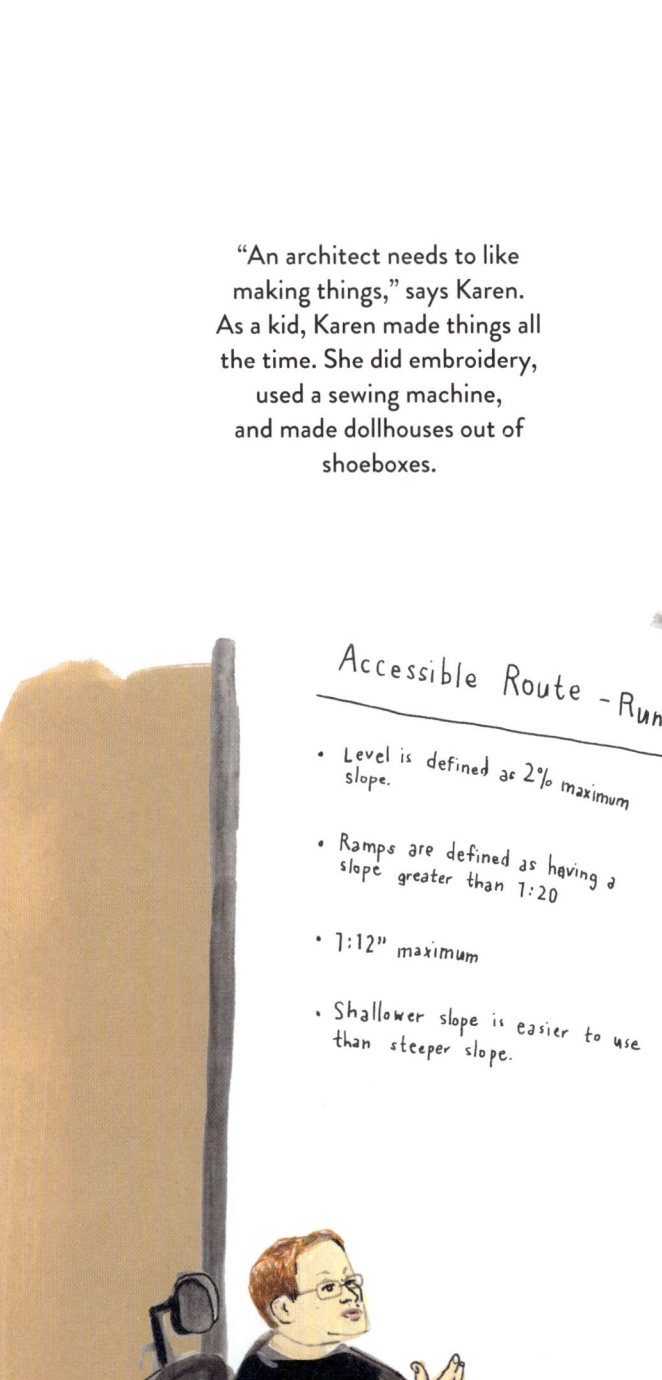

Accessible Route - Running Slope

- Level is defined as 2% maximum slope.

- Ramps are defined as having a slope greater than 1:20

- 1:12" maximum

- Shallower slope is easier to use than steeper slope.

"There's a wide variety of things that can help people better use a building," Karen says. "When members of the Deaf community communicate through **sign language**, they want to be able to walk alongside each other so that they can see each other." Because of that, Karen wants to make sure that hallways are wide enough for people to walk and gesture comfortably.

Karen loves what she does. "I'm making things better for my community and the communities I'm impacting."

? **What can you do to make things better for your community?**

Anpu Varkey is a
MURALIST
based in Bangalore, India.

Anpu rarely paints with a brush—instead, she uses **paint rollers.** "That way it has a lot of texture and I can cover a lot of ground."

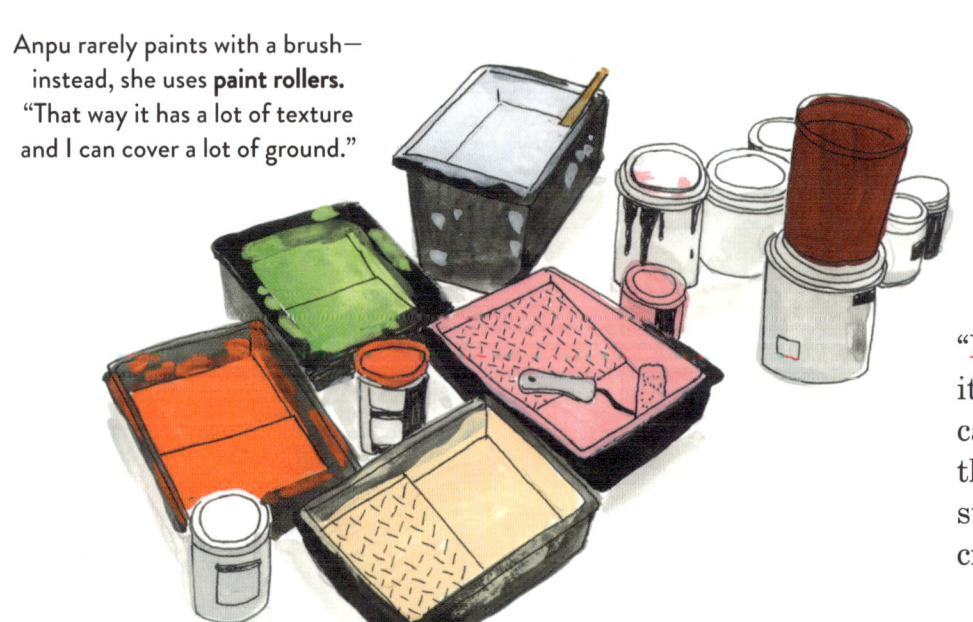

Anpu paints **murals** on the sides of buildings. She has even painted murals on schools. Sometimes people hire her, and sometimes she paints for free.

"I am really quick, so I can do it really fast," says Anpu. "I can do a sixty-foot painting in three days. I paint in a loose style. Very drippy. I like to create textures on the walls."

Anpu sketches the mural out first with watered-down paints. That way, if she makes a mistake, she can correct it.

Painting murals is not a job for someone who is afraid of heights. "You have to do a lot of climbing," says Anpu. "You have to come down and go up a lot while you are painting, because it's hard to see what you're doing when you're up the ladder."

As a kid, Anpu climbed trees. "It brought me a lot of joy," she says. Anpu gets the same amount of joy now when she paints murals. "I enjoy being up a ladder and waving out to people.

"Standing out on the street and painting makes me happy," she says. "A lot of people come by and tell me stories about their life. People come and bring me food and drinks. They bring their little kids and say, 'See how she paints? Maybe you want to paint like that!'"

? Do you like to climb? What do you like to paint? If you were asked to paint on the side of a building, what would you paint?

Nate Macabuag is a

PROSTHETICS MAKER

in London, England.

A prosthetic limb is an **artificial** device that someone wears in place of a limb or to add extra function to their limb. Many people wear prosthetic limbs: some people are born with limbs that are different from most people's, and others may have accidents and lose their limbs later in life. Most prosthetic limbs are hard and **robotic**. "But humans are squishy, so the prosthetics we make are comfy and squishy," says Nate. "People have to enjoy wearing them."

Great for holding bike handlebars or pushing shopping carts

For gripping mugs, drinking glasses, and other wide objects

For strumming instruments such as a guitar

Holds pens, paintbrushes, cooking utensils, and other objects

Holds thin items such as a book or mobile phone

Holds hockey sticks, table tennis paddles, and more

For doing yoga or weight-bearing exercises such as push-ups

The prosthetics come in a backpack with a range of attachments to choose from. Nate and his team ship these backpacks to people all over the world.

Nate doesn't use prosthetics himself, "so I listen to the people who actually use them," he says. Nate meets people with limb differences and tries to understand what it is that they want to do.

The prosthetic arm that Nate designed attaches to the elbow. Then different tools clip into that arm so that people can do different things. "We've designed loads of gizmos and gadgets," says Nate. "There's one for playing a guitar, riding a bike, drawing, doing yoga, holding a **tablet**. To be able to give someone something that they didn't have access to before—it's a good feeling."

? **What kind of gadget would you invent to help make something easier for others?**

Kwangho Lee is a
DESIGNER
in Seoul,
South Korea.

Kwangho designs objects and spaces. He has made stools, tables, light fixtures, sculptures, and more.

Kwangho works with all kinds of materials. He especially likes to work with nylon, leather, wood, **PVC**, and **rice straw**. "I pick a material and I try to make something with it. I'll play with the material, and then I'll find the right shape and technique for it."

Kwangho is inspired by his three children. "We draw together," he says, "or we will go out in the forest and make something together using natural materials."

Many of Kwangho's objects are knitted. "I love to knit," he says. "You start with just one knot, but then you keep going and making it bigger and bigger."

Kwangho designed an entire store using many kinds of materials—from the outside of the building to everything inside, including the door handles, mirrors, lamps, hooks, and even the floor. It took him almost ten months to do it all. "It was quite a big job!" says Kwangho.

Kwangho works mostly using his hands instead of using machines and tools. These chairs are knitted by hand.

? Do you like to build things? What materials have you used? Duct tape? Cardboard? Glue?

Ayesha Rascoe is a
RADIO HOST
in Washington, DC.

Millions of people listen to the show. "I am always nervous when I do the show," says Ayesha. "It's a lot of things you can mess up. You not only have to read the words from the script; you also have to watch the clock while you're doing it!"

"I host a national news show on the radio," says Ayesha. "I guide people through the news on Sunday mornings."

The show that Ayesha hosts is called *Weekend Edition* on NPR. For two hours every Sunday, she helps people figure out what's going on in the world.

"I have to be very careful about how I sound," she says. "If it's a happy story, I have to bring some energy and be happy. But if it's a sad story, I have to be serious. But I still have to be energetic, because you want people to be drawn in by what you're saying."

Ayesha does a lot of vocal exercises before she goes on the radio to warm up her vocal cords, her lips, and her mouth. She does **tongue twisters** to get ready to read the **script** on air. She says "calla yella, walla yella" over and over very fast. "It's hard to get all of the words out when you're talking," she says. "It's actually much harder than it seems!"

Ayesha talks to all kinds of people for her job. "You have to be very curious about people and the world. You have to love asking questions to do what I do."

? What are your favorite questions to ask? Have you ever done a tongue twister?

Tania Esteban is a

WILDLIFE FILMMAKER
based in Bristol, England.

Tania travels all over the world to film animals in nature. The footage she takes becomes wildlife **documentaries**.

Before filming anything, Tania does a lot of research and planning.

Once she is ready to film, Tania wakes up early in the morning to set up her cameras. She dresses in head-to-toe camouflage so that she can blend in with the surroundings, and then she hides so she won't disturb the animals.

Tania spends a long time filming each animal. "You have to be incredibly patient and persistent to be a wildlife filmmaker," she says.

"There are incredible animals on this planet that have important lives," says Tania. "These animals are trying to find mates, make homes, get food." Tania wants people to feel a sense of wonder at how amazing the world is. "I want people to appreciate how lucky we are to live on a planet with such incredible **biodiversity**."

Tania hopes that if people feel connected to nature, they will do a better job taking care of it.

? What kinds of cool animals and birds do you see in your community? Have you ever taken photos of them or drawn them?

Tania has filmed all kinds of animals, including orangutans, ostriches, bowerbirds, and the blue-footed booby.

Aubry and **Kale Walch** are

VEGAN BUTCHERS

in **Minneapolis, Minnesota.**

"We grew up in Guam in a family that ate a lot of meat," says Aubry. "But I became a vegan when I was fourteen and then Kale when he was sixteen."

At their store, The Herbivorous Butcher, the **siblings** sell **vegan** products that look like meat and taste like meat but are made of plants—like wheat or garbanzo beans. They do this to save animals.

When they first got started, Kale and Aubry experimented in the kitchen to see if they could make **plant-based meat** that tasted yummy. After trying many different recipes, they found some that worked!

"We discovered that by blending different juices, spices, and vinegars, you can get anything from Italian sausage to a ribeye steak," says Kale. "Our steaks are made using garbanzo flour and red wine vinegar, which helps make them very tender. Our chicken recipe uses white flour—which creates strands—so that the finished product shreds like real chicken."

Kale and Aubry are always trying to come up with new recipes. And it still takes a lot of experimentation. "I'll go through five failed batches before we get the recipe just right," says Kale.

? **What kind of experimenting have you done in the kitchen? Have you ever tried plant-based meat?**

Chef Fresh is a
FARMER & CHEF
in Chicago, Illinois.

"I live, farm, and work all on the South Side of Chicago," says Chef Fresh. "Most of the work I do is feeding my community.

"The farm that I'm currently on is a seven-**acre** farm." Chef Fresh shares that farm with other farmers. "You can produce a lot of food on a small amount of land." On that farm, they grow garlic, onions, peppers, celery, beans, and lots of herbs.

"My favorite meal is breakfast," says Chef Fresh. "I love when I get to make breakfast for dinner."

Chef Fresh works with three other cooks to provide 350 meals a week to people in need. "We've done about thirty thousand meals at this point," says the chef. "Every Wednesday I'm in the kitchen all day making meals for folks who need them."

After the meals are made, they get labeled and put into bags. Then the meals get distributed in the community.

As a kid, Chef Fresh liked being in the kitchen. "I liked seeing my grandma cook. I always wanted to help."

? If you had to make a whole meal for someone, what would you cook? Do you ever volunteer in your community?

I Chen is an

ALPACA FARMER

in Akaroa, New Zealand.

"Our farm is one hundred acres big," says I. "Right now, we have around one hundred and sixty alpacas on the farm. We always want to have under two hundred so we don't run out of grass." Alpacas mainly eat grass or hay, but sometimes I has to prepare special food for an alpaca who is ill or elderly.

Every day, I makes sure the alpacas are healthy and happy and he cleans out their **paddocks**. He also gives tours to people visiting the farm.

"We **shear** the alpacas once a year," says I. "Normally we do it right before summer. In New Zealand, summertime is from December to February." After the alpacas are shorn, the farm makes knitwear out of the fleece and then sells that knitwear in a shop on the farm.

On the farm, every single alpaca has a name. "We have one named Rising Sun, another is Sakura, another is Tia Maria. And then we have one who is named Dennis."

? **What kinds of animals do you like to take care of? Have you ever worn clothing made out of alpaca fleece?**

Alpacas are known for being very soft. "They have a very fine fleece," says I. "Unlike sheep, their fleece doesn't have any oil on it, so after you've been petting them or cuddling them, you won't smell a thing."

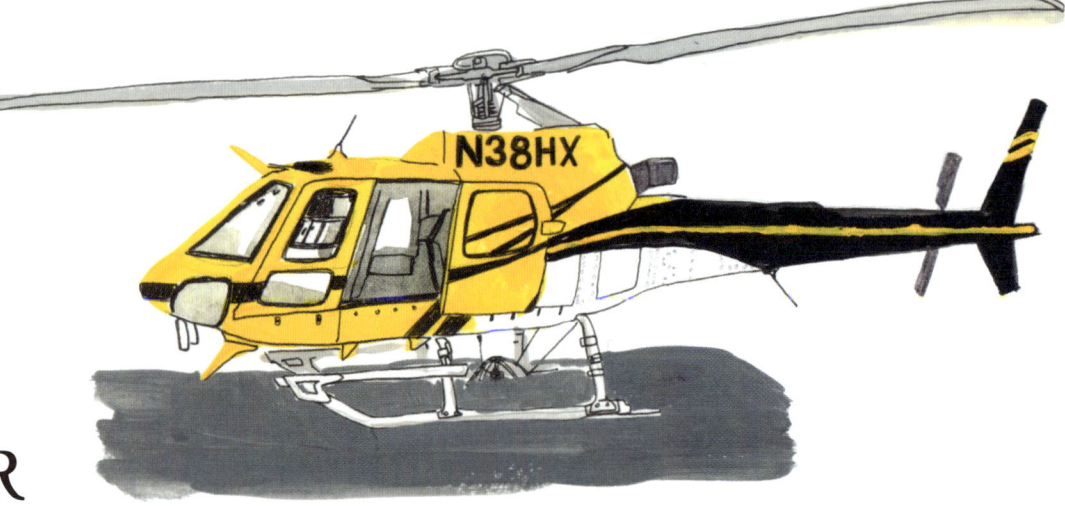

Mary Lee is a

WILDLAND FIREFIGHTER

based in Jackson, Wyoming.

"I am in charge of a **squad** of firefighters," says Mary.

When **dispatchers** receive reports of a wildfire, they alert firefighters like Mary. Then Mary and her crew have to get to the fire. "We get in the helicopter and most of the time we see smoke and we fly toward it," says Mary.

When she is working, Mary wears fireproof clothing and a flight helmet.

Mary always carries water and snacks in her bag.

Once Mary and her crew land, they start fighting the fire. Sometimes that means getting people on the ground to start digging **trenches** around the fire. And sometimes it means dropping water on the fire from the helicopter using special buckets.

Mary is very brave, but she says she doesn't feel like a hero. "It does feel amazing," says Mary, "that a group of people are able to work really hard to make a difference."

? **When were you brave?**

Peter Schultze is a

FERRY CAPTAIN

on the Weser River in Germany.

The ferry transports people, bikes, motorbikes, cars, and sometimes **oversize vehicles** from one town to another.

Some days, Peter does up to seventy-six trips across the river. "The trip is very short," he says. "It only takes three to four minutes."

For the first five years of his life, Peter lived on a boat.

The hardest part of Peter's job is dealing with weather. "If there are high winds, it can be tough to steer the boat," he says. "But even worse than wind is fog." If it is very foggy, it is hard to **dock** the boat.

When there is another boat on the river, Peter waves at the people on that boat. He does a specific wave—he moves his hand twice to the right and once to the left. Sometimes, Peter will even toot the horn at that boat. But he tries not to toot the horn too much because it is noisy.

Many years ago, Peter saw something surprising from the ferry. "There were three **porpoises** in the river," he says. "It was very unusual because there aren't normally porpoises in the water. I wasn't sure if I was **hallucinating**! But other people on the ferry saw them, too."

Twenty-two regular-size cars can fit on the ferry.

? **Can you do Peter's wave? Do you like to travel by boat, plane, or car?**

Mamie Minch and **Chloë Swantner** are

LUTHIERS

in Brooklyn, New York.

A luthier is someone who builds or repairs **stringed instruments**. Mamie and Chloë have worked on many instruments, including guitars, ukuleles, violins, and violas.

People come into Mamie and Chloë's shop with instruments that need repair. Some of the repairs are big—Mamie and Chloë will have to pull apart an entire guitar. Some of the repairs are teeny-tiny—they will have to use a magnifying glass and a three-haired paintbrush.

Sometimes, the instruments they work on are very unique. "We have a client who plays a traditional instrument from **Chechnya**," says Mamie. "It looks like a small banjo, but the skin of it comes from the third **chamber** of a camel's heart!"

"You often have to make a tool to fix the instrument," says Chloë. It takes a lot of creative problem solving to be a luthier.

"There are no guitar emergencies," says Mamie. "Instruments are made out of wood and metal—if they break, you fix them!"

After they fix each instrument, Mamie and Chloë sit down and play them to make sure they sound good.

? **What is your favorite instrument to play? Why?**

Patrice Banks is an

AUTO TECHNICIAN

in Upper Darby, Pennsylvania.

Before becoming an **auto technician**, Patrice didn't know anything about cars. "Anytime anything would happen with my car, I would panic. I always felt like I needed a guy to help me. I hated my experiences when it came to my car. Not very empowering."

"Auto technicians are problem solvers," says Patrice. "When something breaks, they have to figure out why, and then they have to fix it!"

She enrolled in school and learned to work on cars. As soon as she learned about repairing cars, she couldn't wait to teach other women those skills. Patrice started Girls Auto Clinic to train other women how to repair cars.

"It feels good to be able to work on cars," says Patrice. "But you know what feels better? Inspiring women. Every day my staff shows up to work, they're inspiring other women to be more confident and to try something they might not have before."

? **What kinds of problems do you like to solve?**

Julia Rothman is an

ILLUSTRATOR

in Brooklyn, New York.

When Julia was a kid, she learned to draw all of her favorite cartoon characters from TV shows.

She is the person who painted all of the pictures in this book. She loves her job because she gets to draw all day.

Julia has a lot of supplies in her studio. She has paintbrushes, markers, pens, erasers, pencil sharpeners, and every color of paint.

"The hardest thing about my job is that sometimes when I draw things, they don't look the way I want them to," says Julia. "You have to just be okay with it. Or you have to fix it a lot."

 **What is your favorite thing to draw?**

Shaina Feinberg is a
WRITER
in Brooklyn, New York.

She wrote this book.

She loves to tell her own stories, and she loves to help other people tell their stories. She also really loves to learn about people.

Sometimes Shaina finds people to interview using the internet. And sometimes she just walks out on the street to talk to people.

"Julia and I go outside and stand on a street corner and we say to people who are walking by, 'Excuse me, can we talk to you?' Some people say no and some people say yes. Every single time they say yes, it's awesome," she says.

? **Have you ever interviewed anyone?**

At the back of this book, you can find interview questions so you can interview someone you know.

Shaina has always loved to ask questions.

HOW WE MADE THIS BOOK

Julia Rothman and Shaina Feinberg have a column in the business section of the *New York Times*. They often talk to small-business owners and people who have interesting jobs. After several years of doing their column, they wanted to make a picture book that is similar to what they do in the newspaper.

Julia and Shaina set out to interview people all over the world who have unique and inspiring jobs. Many of the people they interviewed were far away, so Julia and Shaina interviewed them on Zoom. Sometimes they interviewed people very late at night because they were talking to someone on the other side of the world. Several times, Julia and Shaina had to use translators to help them communicate in different languages, like Spanish, German, Japanese, and Italian.

After the interviews, Shaina wrote up what the people said and Julia painted them by looking at photographs.

If you'd like to do something similar to what Julia and Shaina do . . .

Try interviewing someone you know. Here are some questions to get you started. Feel free to come up with some of your own, too!

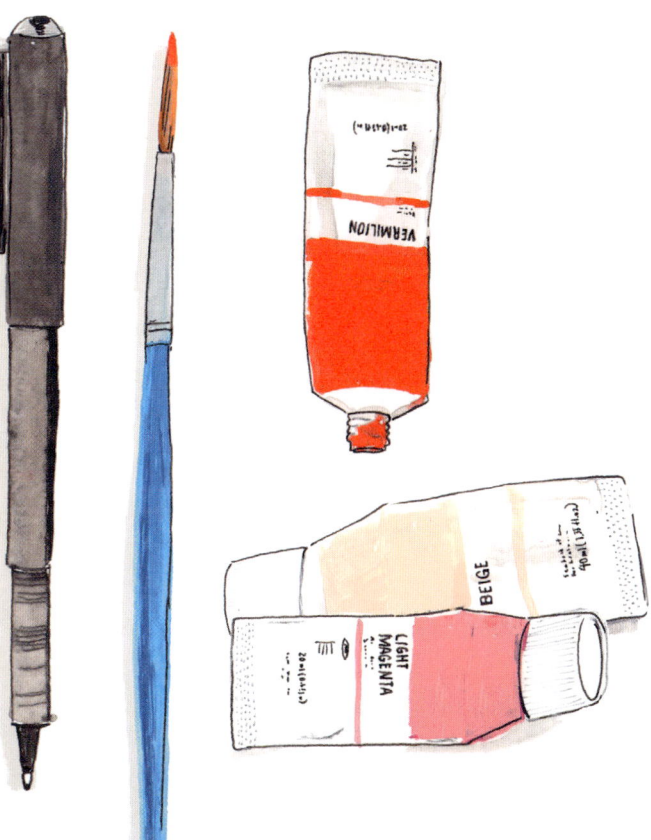

Try painting someone you know. Julia likes to look at photographs as she paints, rather than painting someone in person. That way the people aren't moving and she can work as slowly as she wants.

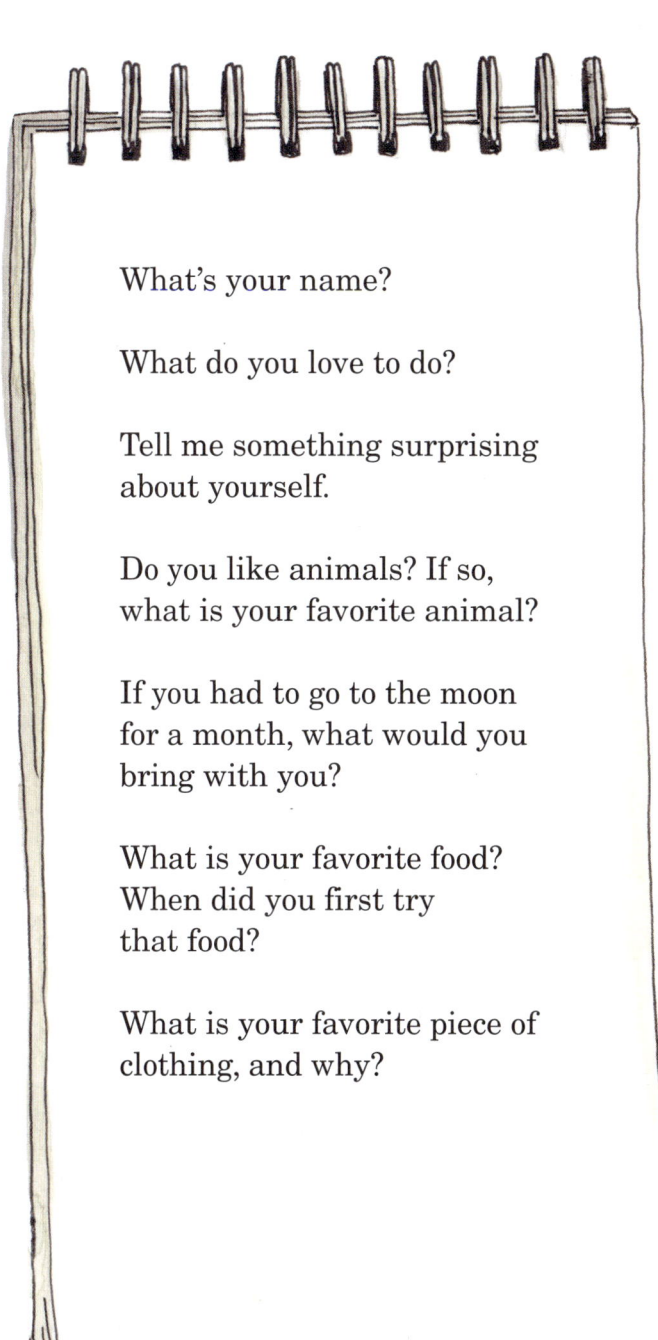

What's your name?

What do you love to do?

Tell me something surprising about yourself.

Do you like animals? If so, what is your favorite animal?

If you had to go to the moon for a month, what would you bring with you?

What is your favorite food? When did you first try that food?

What is your favorite piece of clothing, and why?

COPYRIGHT ACKNOWLEDGMENTS

Many of the illustrations in this book were based on or inspired by photographs. The illustrator gratefully acknowledges the photographers who created those images:

p. 6 Photograph copyright © 2018 by Musiime P. Muramura (Robert Aruho)

p. 10 Photograph copyright © 2022 by Andini Makosinski (Andini Makosinski)

pp. 12–13 Photographs copyright © 2021 by Pete Kern (Pete Kern)

pp. 14–15 Photographs copyright © 2022 by Budj Bim National Park (Braydon Saunders)

pp. 16–17 Story/illustration inspired by or featuring ST-VIATEUR BAGEL. All rights reserved. (Joe Morena)

p. 18 Photograph (top) copyright © 2014 by Vitor Estrelinha (Joana Andrade)

p. 18 Photograph (portrait, bottom) copyright © 2021 by Tassio Pniewski (Joana Andrade)

p. 19 Photograph (top) copyright © 2021 by Tassio Pniewski (Joana Andrade)

p. 19 Photograph (bottom) copyright © 2019 by Tim Bonython (Joana Andrade)

pp. 20–21 Photographs copyright © 2021 by Lilian Fotografie (Linda van der Slot and Marlies Weijers)

pp. 22–23 Photographs copyright © 2022 by Isaac Tobin (Lauren Nassef)

pp. 24–25 Photographs copyright © 2021 by Fabian Uset (Pato Rodriguez)

pp. 26–27 Photographs copyright © 2017, 2018, 2023 by Iman Aldebe (Iman Aldebe)

p. 28 Photograph (left) copyright © 2022 by Bea Borgers (Satoko Ichihara)

p. 29 Photograph (group photo) copyright © 2019 by Yuichiro Yoshida, courtesy of Kinosaki International Arts Center (Toyooka City) (Satoko Ichihara)

pp. 30–31 Photographs copyright © 2022 by Silvano Arnoldo (Daniela Ghezzo)

pp. 32–33 Photographs copyright © 2013, 2018, 2019 by Karen L. Braitmayer, Studio Pacifica (Karen Braitmayer)

p. 34 Photograph (portrait) copyright © 2021 by RS Gopan (Anpu Varkey)

p. 35 Photographs copyright © 2020 by Anpu Varkey (Anpu Varkey)

pp. 36–37 Photographs copyright © 2021, 2022 by Koalaa (Nate Macabuag)

p. 38 Photograph copyright © 2022 by Jihoon Kang (Kwangho Lee)

p. 39 Photograph copyright © 2022 by Kwangho Lee (Kwangho Lee)

p. 40 Photograph copyright © 2022 by Ted Mebane (Ayesha Rascoe)

p. 41 Photograph copyright © 2022 by Ayesha Rascoe (Ayesha Rascoe)

pp. 42–43 Photographs copyright © 2021 by Peter Cayless (Tania Esteban)

p. 44 Photograph (portrait, top left) copyright © 2014 by Daniel Campbell (The Herbivorous Butcher)

p. 44 Photograph (bottom) copyright © 2015 by The Herbivorous Butcher (The Herbivorous Butcher)

p. 45 Photograph (top and middle) copyright © 2015 by The Herbivorous Butcher (The Herbivorous Butcher)

p. 45 Photograph (bottom) copyright © 2014 by Daniel Campbell (The Herbivorous Butcher)

p. 46 Photographs copyright © 2022 by Bennet Goldstein (Chef Fresh)

p. 47 Photograph copyright © 2019 by Shulamis Rouzaud (Chef Fresh, with dough machine)

p. 47 Photograph copyright © 2022 by Nuatoshia Price (Chef Fresh, ladling food)

p. 47 Photographs (yellow container, paper bags) copyright © 2022 by Bennet Goldstein

p. 48 Photograph (portrait, top left) copyright © 2022 by Johannes Brunner (I Chen)

pp. 48–49 Photographs copyright © 2022 by Anya Walkington (I Chen)

pp. 50–51 Photographs copyright © 2015–2017, 2019, 2021 by Mary Lee (Mary Lee)

pp. 52–53 Photographs copyright © 2022 by Peter Schultze (Peter Schultze)

pp. 56–57 Photographs copyright © 2018 by Patrice Banks and Girls Auto Clinic (Patrice Banks)